ABOUT THE BANK STREET READY-TO-READ SERIES

Seventy-five years of educational research and innovative teaching have given the Bank Street College of Education the reputation as America's most trusted name in early childhood education.

Because no two children are exactly alike in their development, we have designed the *Bank Street Ready-to-Read* series in three levels to accommodate the individual stages of reading readiness of children ages four through eight.

- ○ *Level 1:* GETTING READY TO READ—read-alouds for children who are taking their first steps toward reading.

- ● *Level 2:* READING TOGETHER—for children who are just beginning to read by themselves but may need a little help.

- ○ *Level 3:* I CAN READ IT MYSELF—for children who can read independently.

Our three levels make it easy to select the books most appropriate for a child's development and enable him or her to grow with the series step by step. The *Bank Street Ready-to-Read* books also overlap and reinforce each other, further encouraging the reading process.

We feel that making reading fun and enjoyable is the single most important thing that you can do to help children become good readers. And we hope you'll be a part of Bank Street's long tradition of learning through sharing.

The Bank Street College of Education

To Byron to read to Karah
—J.O.
To Cara, Eliza, and Dana
—C.D.

"UH-OH!" SAID THE CROW

A Bantam Book/November 1993

Published by Bantam Doubleday Dell Books for Young Readers,
a division of Bantam Doubleday Dell Publishing Group, Inc.
1540 Broadway, New York, New York 10036

Series graphic design by Alex Jay/Studio J

*Special thanks to James A. Levine, Betsy Gould,
and Diane Arico.*

*The trademarks "Bantam Books" and the portrayal of a rooster
are registered in the U.S. Patent and Trademark Office and in
other countries. Marca Registrada.*

Library of Congress Cataloging-in-Publication Data
Oppenheim, Joanne.
"Uh-oh!" said the crow / by Joanne Oppenheim ;
illustrated by Chris Demarest.
p.   cm.—(Bank Street ready-to-read)
"A Byron Preiss book."
"A Bantam book."
Summary: On a dark and windy night,
the animals in the barn are frightened
by strange noises above them
and think there might be a ghost
in the barn with them.
ISBN 0-553-09387-8.—ISBN 0-553-37186-X
[1. Domestic animals—Fiction.   2. Sound—Fiction.]
I. Demarest, Chris L., ill.   II. Title.   III. Series.
PZ7.O616Uh   1993
[E]—dc20   92-1629   CIP   AC

Published simultaneously in the United States and Canada

PRINTED IN THE UNITED STATES OF AMERICA

0 9 8 7 6 5 4 3 2 1

"Uh·Oh!" Said the Crow

by Joanne Oppenheim
Illustrated by Chris Demarest

A Byron Preiss Book

A BANTAM BOOK

WHOOOO!
It was a dark and windy night.
In the barn, all the animals
were sound asleep.

Just before dawn there was
a terrible THUD!
"Uh-oh!" cawed Crow.

5

"What was that?" mewed Cat.
"I don't know," cawed Crow.
"It's up there," whinnied Mare.
As she pointed to the loft,
there was another loud THUD!

"Uh-oh!" cawed Crow.
"What was that?" mewed Cat.
"It's up there," whinnied Mare.
"Sounds like spooks!" honked Goose.

Now the whistling wind
swept around the barn
calling WHOOO! WHOOOO!
And from the loft
came the frightening sound of
THUD!
     THUD!
        THUD!

"Uh-oh!" cawed Crow.

"Might be a ghost!" bleated Goat.

"Don't say that!" mewed Cat.

"It's up there," whinnied Mare.

"Must be spooks!" honked Goose.
"What bad luck!" quacked Duck.
"Go back to sleep," baaed Sheep.

But Crow, Goat, Cat, Mare,
Goose, and Duck
were too scared to sleep.
They sat side by side, shaking with fear.

"I know," cawed Crow.
"Someone has to go up in the loft
to see what's there."
"I'm afraid!" Donkey brayed.

Again the wind cried
WHOOO! WHOOOOO!
And a loud and terrible
THUD!
         THUD!
                   THUD!
rumbled from above.

"What now?" mooed Cow.
"Might be a ghost!" bleated Goat.
"Don't say that!" mewed Cat.
"It's up there," whinnied Mare.

"Who will go?" cawed Crow.

"Nix! Nix!" peeped the Chicks.

"Sounds like spooks!"
honked Goose.

"Go back to sleep," baaed Sheep.

Crow tried to stay calm.
But now all the animals
in the barn
were wide awake and worrying.

Crow thought and thought.

Finally he had an idea.
"Let's draw straws.
The one who draws the longest
must go up to see what's there."

"Not my job!" grunted Hog.
"Nix! Nix!" peeped the Chicks.
"Not right now!" mooed Cow.
"No such luck," quacked Duck.
"I'm afraid!" Donkey brayed.

Again the wind howled
WHOO! WHOOO!
And something overhead went
THUD!
    THUD!
        THUMP!
"It's a ghost!" bleated Goat.
"It's up there," whinnied Mare.
"What bad luck!" quacked Duck.
"Sounds like spooks!" honked Goose.
"Don't say that!" mewed Cat.
"Go back to sleep," baaed Sheep.

"Uh-oh!" cawed Crow.
"I guess I know who has to go."

And saying that,
Crow gathered up his courage,
spread his wings,
and disappeared into the dark loft above.

Hog, Cow, Duck, Donkey, Goat, Mare,
Goose, Cat, Sheep, and the Chicks
sat as still as stones,
waiting and listening.

24

All at once there was a storm
of THUDS and THUMPS
and Crow began to caw,
"Uh-oh! Oh, no!"

And hearing Crow,
they all ran for the door—
mooing and grunting,
baaing and peeping,
mewing and braying,
honking and bleating.

And running outside,
they heard the thudding sound
as the wind hit the apples
that hit the barn
that hit the ground!

And up in the treetop
they saw brave Crow
jumping on the branches, cawing,
"WATCH OUT BELOW!"

"Some ghost," bleated Goat.
"So much for spooks!" honked Goose.
"Such a scare!" whinnied Mare.
"What good luck!" quacked Duck.
"I saved the show!" cawed Crow.

"Glad I stayed!" Donkey brayed.
"Let's eat!" baaed Sheep.
"I'm for that!" mewed Cat.
"Right now!" mooed Cow.
"That's my job!" grunted Hog.
"First picks!" peeped the Chicks.

So all that day and into the night
they munched and crunched apples
till the moon turned bright.
They munched and crunched apples
one by one,
they munched and crunched apples
until there were none.

32